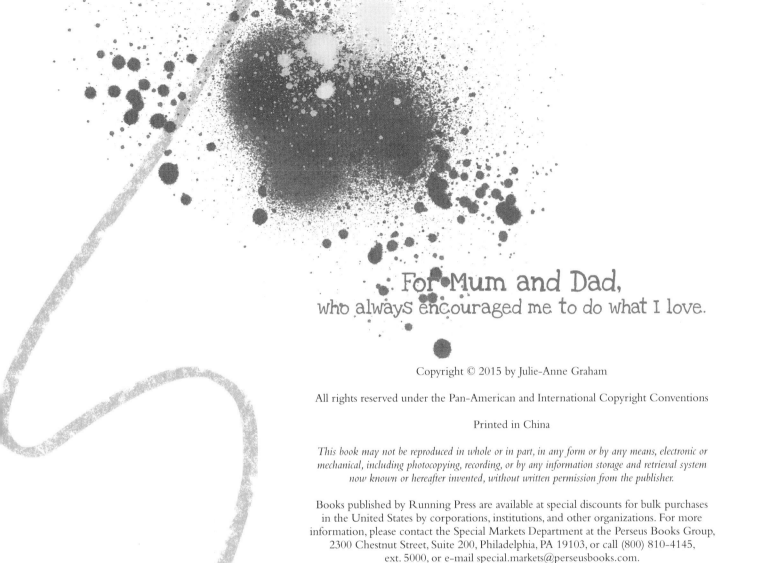

For Mum and Dad,
who always encouraged me to do what I love.

Books published by Running Press are available at special discounts for bulk purchases in the United States by corporations, institutions, and other organizations. For more information, please contact the Special Markets Department at the Perseus Books Group, 2300 Chestnut Street, Suite 200, Philadelphia, PA 19103, or call (800) 810-4145, ext. 5000, or e-mail special.markets@perseusbooks.com.

ISBN 978-0-7624-5506-5
Library of Congress Control Number: 2014942576

9 8 7 6 5 4 3 2 1
Digit on the right indicates the number of this printing

Edited by Lisa Cheng
Typography: Bembo, LBSweetie Bold, Love Ya Like a Sister

Published by Running Press Kids
An Imprint of Running Press Book Publishers
A Member of the Perseus Books Group
2300 Chestnut Street
Philadelphia, PA 19103–4371

Visit us on the web!
www.runningpress.com/rpkids

The Perfect Percival Priggs

by Julie-Anne Graham

Percival Priggs was perfect.
His parents were perfect.
His grandparents were perfect.
Even his pets were perfect.

They each had a shelf to display their awards . . .

... and they were always competing for more.

Percy found the business of
being perfect quite exhausting!

But he was scared that his parents
wouldn't love him if he wasn't.

So he said nothing.

And if you ever asked him how he was, he would smile his prize-winning smile and say,

I'm perfect. Thank you.

One weekend, the family was hard at work preparing for their upcoming competitions.

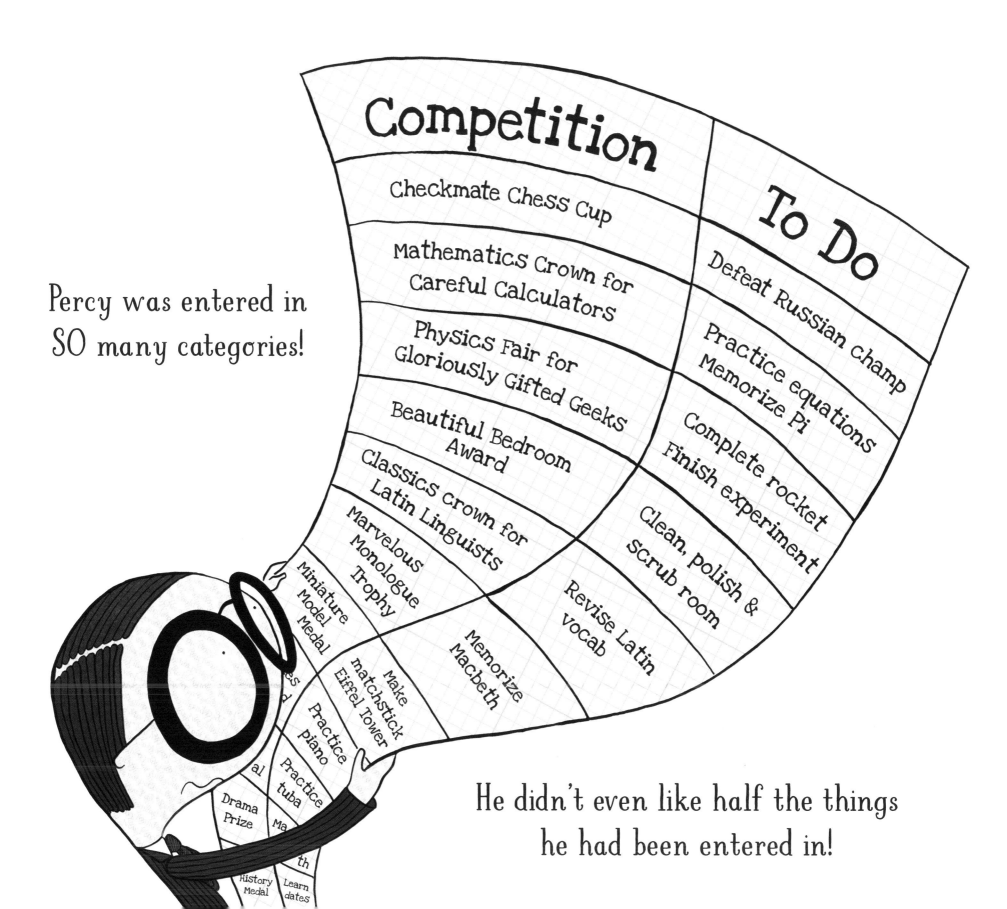

Percy was entered in SO many categories!

Competition

Checkmate Chess Cup

Mathematics Crown for Careful Calculators

Physics Fair for Gloriously Gifted Geeks

Beautiful Bedroom Award

Classics Crown for Latin Linguists

Marvelous Monologue Trophy

Miniature Model Medal

Make matchstick Eiffel Tower

Memorize Macbeth

Practice piano

Practice tuba

Drama Prize

Ma...th

History Medal

Learn dates

To Do

Defeat Russian champ

Practice equations Memorize Pi

Complete rocket Finish experiment

Clean, polish & scrub room

Revise Latin vocab

He didn't even like half the things he had been entered in!

So he came up with a plan to finish faster . . .

But he made a slight miscalculation . . .

Percy's rocket was definitely not perfect.

And now neither was anything else!

His parents were going to be furious.

"Your father didn't win any prizes for this experiment!" Mrs. Priggs said.

"And your mother's coconut and chili cake wasn't exactly a hit," said Mr. Priggs.

"This was your father a week after he won the Spick-and-Span Car Award!"

"And your mother's first piano recital didn't go too well."

"Then your father wore the wrong glasses to the Heavenly Hedges competition."

"And your mother's dog training didn't always go as planned."

So Percy
found
things
he
loved.

And he tried . . .

And tried again . . .

And failed . . .

Now Percy's shelf looks a lot different.

But his favorite award of all is
one he didn't need to earn.